A Novel
Written by Dina Anastasio

Based on the Motion Picture Screenplay
Written by Alan Shapiro

SCHOLASTIC INC.
New York Toronto London Auckland Sydney

FOR ELIZA
—D. A.

ISBN 0-590-13177-X

12 11 10 9 8 7 6 5 4 3 2 1   6 7 8 9/9 0 1/0

Printed in the U.S.A.   40

First Scholastic printing, September 1996

Chapter 1

Sandy Burns punched some numbers on his phone and dropped down onto his bed. His friend, Joel, picked up after the first ring.

"So?" Joel asked. "Are we in?"

Sandy laughed. He knew his friend had been sitting by the phone since dawn. He decided to drag out the suspense for as long as he could. "OK. So I'm surfing all night on the Net and—"

"Come on, man," Joel interrupted impatiently. "Just tell me if you got it or not!"

"As I was saying, I bust in on the Red Hot Chili Peppers forum. The tour manager's girlfriend was looking for some freebies at this health spa, just like we thought she would. It looked like she'd do anything, so—"

"Did you get it, Sandy?!" Joel was dying to know.

"Well, I surfed some more and got them for her, did some trading here and there, and in return . . ." Sandy paused.

"Yeah? And?" Joel was really getting annoyed now.

"So, she asked what she could do for me, and I said, well, how about a couple of all-access laminates—you know, to get us back stage so we could meet the group!"

"No kidding!"

"And what do you think she said?" Sandy teased.

"No, of course."

Sandy laughed. Then he laid it on him. "In fact, 'yes' is what she happened to say. So, we're in. All access to the Red Hot Chili Peppers concert."

"NO WAY!"

"Yup. We're going on stage. We're going to the party after. We're gonna hang with Flea! With my mom going away, and my Grandma staying here, we can—" A knock on his door stopped him. "Just a minute!" Sandy shouted.

"Sandy?" It was his mother's voice. "We need to talk."

"Can you wait a second? I'm on the phone."

"SANDY!" She didn't sound happy.

Sandy sighed and told Joel that he'd call him back. Then he strolled across the room and opened the door. "What's up?" he mumbled, trying not to sound irritated.

"It's about your summer plans," his mom said.

"What about them?" Sandy was starting to feel a little queasy.

His mother was heading for his bed. When she sat down, he knew that this was going to be a long conversation.

"Grandma broke her hip getting in the tub," she explained once she was settled on the bed.

"Is she OK?" Sandy asked.

His mother took off her shoes and tucked her feet up under her. This was going to be a very long conversation.

"She'll be fine. But she won't be coming to stay with you," she added.

"I can stay here alone," Sandy answered confidently.

This was all right. In fact, this was great. The perfect summer.

His mom folded her arms and looked up at Sandy. "I'm not comfortable with that. Not while I'm gone. You're fourteen, you know, and ever since your father left you spend all your time at the mall. You don't seem to care about school anymore. You treat your sister like a stranger—"

"You're not sending me back to that stupid summer camp!" Sandy cried. "There's no way I'm going back there!"

His mom shook her head. "No, I'm not. Not that they'd take you after the stunt you pulled up there. Sandy, do you remember me telling you about my sister's ex-husband? Your Uncle Porter?"

Sandy's eyes widened as he recalled what had been said about Uncle Porter. "You mean the lowlife deadbeat? The loser? The hippie dropout?"

His mother frowned. "Those are your aunt's words."

"I thought you said Uncle Porter got lost looking for himself, or something," Sandy replied.

"He used to teach. But now he lives on an island and fishes. I think you'll like him," she said enthusiastically. "He's different. And personally, I think he's interesting. He used to be a professional surfer, you know."

But Sandy wasn't listening. He was thinking about his summer. So Uncle Porter would be staying with him while his mom was away. That might be all right. Maybe.

"Well, I don't care if he's different," Sandy said. "As long as he uses your bathroom while he's here."

"Uncle Porter's not coming to Chicago, Sandy," his mother said.

At first Sandy didn't get it. It took several minutes to register. And when it finally did, he didn't just feel queasy anymore, he felt definitely sick. "You mean . . . I'm going *there*?"

"That's right. You'll like it, Sandy. You can help him fish. And you'll learn a lot about nature. You know, things you'll never learn about here in Chicago!" His mom had a nervous smile on her face—as if she was trying to convince herself at the same time she was trying to convince Sandy.

Nature? Sandy thought. Nature? Was she kidding? No, he could

tell from her face that she was dead serious. She'd already made up her mind. This was going to be a terrible summer. In fact, it could just be the worst summer of his whole, entire life.

✿ ✿ ✿

A week later Sandy was standing in front of their condo with his duffle bag in his hand. He was still feeling sick, but now he knew there was nothing he could do about it. He had tried everything. He had begged. He had pleaded. He had done everything but get down on his hands and knees. But nothing had worked. His mom held firm.

"Well, I guess this is good-bye, Sandy," she said, leaning in to hug him.

But Sandy wasn't having any of that. He was furious. When he saw what his mom was going to do, he stepped back and glared at her.

She hesitated. Then she turned away. Sandy could see that he had hurt her feelings. But he didn't care.

His mom shook her head and sighed. "Lately you don't seem to care about anything except yourself. Maybe this will be a good thing. Maybe some time at Uncle Porter's will do you good. Try to think of it as a new beginning."

When she leaned over to kiss him, Sandy tensed but didn't budge. Then he shrugged it off as if none of it mattered and walked toward the cab.

The driver was waiting. He reached for Sandy's bag, but Sandy wasn't having any of that either. He was perfectly able to take care of his own bag, thank you very much.

He slid into the cab without looking at his mom. As the driver started the engine, Sandy closed his eyes and thought about the Red Hot Chili Peppers concert. He didn't know where he was going. He didn't know what would happen to him. But there was one thing that he did know: No matter what happened, he was still going to that concert. There was no doubt about that!

Chapter 2

When the ferry docked at the island, Sandy took his time. There was no point in hurrying. It was going to be a too-long summer anyway, so why start it too soon? If Porter was on the dock, he'd just have to wait.

But Porter wasn't on the dock. Sandy milled around for a long time before he realized that no one at all was there to meet him. He searched the crowd for someone, anyone, but everyone was hugging and chattering away with each other. No one was holding a sign with his name. No one was calling him. No one was even looking for him. No one.

He waited until everyone was gone, just to make sure. And then he started down a dusty dirt road that meandered along the ocean.

It was a beautiful island. Wildflowers and butterflies lined the road. But it was so quiet. Too quiet. It was a nowhere place. That was obvious. What was he going to do here for one whole, long, summer?

He had been walking for a long time when the sound of gulls made him hesitate. He looked for them, couldn't find them, then realized they were right in front of him hiding on a filthy mailbox by the side of the road.

"WELCOME TO RICK'S PLACE—Porter Ricks, Proprietor," read the sign by the mailbox. So this was it. His new home. He looked around and groaned. The ramshackle hovel that passed for a house was even worse than the mailbox. He surveyed the area surrounding it. The white sand beach was all right. And so was the small dock. But the house was a wretched mess. It didn't even look fit to live in.

Sandy groaned again and dropped his duffle bag. He was thinking about going back to the ferry when a pelican clomped up and looked him over. Sandy stepped back.

The bird studied him a little longer, squawked, and waddled down to the water. Sandy watched him go. Then he turned and tip-toed onto the porch.

"Hello?" Sandy called softly as he opened the door.

The inside of the house was even worse than he had expected. The place was covered with dust. Old chicken bones littered a table and rested on the arm of a chair. A lizard watched him from on top of the TV. It was terrible. And it was empty.

The gunning sound of a boat's motor brought him back outside. One glance at the boat told him all he needed to know. This was his Uncle Porter. A young woman was in the driver's seat, and she was pulling him on water skis. He was dressed in loud Hawaiian shorts, and he was drinking a beer. There was no doubt about it. His uncle was everything his parents had joked about in private when they thought he wasn't listening.

As Sandy walked down toward the dock, the pelican fluttered out of the water. The bird was frantic. He wanted something. But what?

"Sit!" Uncle Porter shouted. "Sit down, Pete!"

Pete sat, and Porter poured some beer into his beak. The bird seemed satisfied.

Of course! Sandy thought. The pelican had just wanted some beer. How silly of him not to have guessed. From the foot of the dock, Sandy called out a tentative, "Hello?"

Porter glanced up and frowned. "Sandy?"

"Uh-huh."

Porter scratched his head. "What are you doing here? I thought you were coming on Thursday."

"It *is* Thursday."

Porter sighed and rolled his eyes. "Guess I missed your boat," he said guiltily. "Well, I'll make it up to you, buddy. You're gonna have one heck of a summer. Just you wait and see."

Porter extended his hand, but Sandy wasn't interested. He didn't want to be there. And he didn't like this guy—at all! "Do me a favor. Don't call me buddy. OK?"

Porter shrugged and headed toward the house. Pete followed. "Heel, Pete," Porter called. The pelican caught up and waddled down the path beside him.

"So where do I sleep?" Sandy asked once he was inside.

"Let's see. I guess you can crash on the couch."

Pete growled an angry growl that shook the small room. Sandy looked at him out of the corner of his eye. Did the bird speak English, too?

Porter laughed. "Then again, you'll probably be more comfortable in the back. Looks like Pete's not about to give up his bed. And who could blame the poor bird?"

The bed in the back was an army cot, and it took a long time to find it. The back room was a war zone. There was junk everywhere. The cot was covered with so many cans of SpaghettiOs that it was almost invisible.

"Like SpaghettiOs much?" Sandy muttered, as he moved the cans aside and dropped his bag on the cot. A soft cloud of dust rose up and covered them both. He turned and glanced over his shoulder. "By the way, how much did she pay you to take me off her hands?"

Porter seemed insulted. But Sandy knew he was faking it. "I resent that," Porter said. "When your mother called, I didn't hesitate.

I figured it'd be a chance to reconnect with the family. Family's important, you know. You should always remember that. You guys are all I've got."

"How much?" Sandy asked again.

"Hundred bucks a week. For expenses."

Sandy shook his head. "Man, she really low-balled you," he groaned. "What a sucker!"

"Story of my life," Porter shrugged. "Story of my entire life, bud—" He caught himself before he finished saying the word. "Sorry. I'll try harder."

They came together again at dinner, over SpaghettiOs. At first they didn't speak, and Sandy would have been happy to keep it that way. He kept thinking about the Red Hot Chili Peppers laminates, and it was making him feel ill.

"Ever been fishing?" Porter said when they were finally finished eating.

"Duh," Sandy groaned, rolling his eyes.

"What'd you catch?"

"A whale. But I threw it back."

"I'm just asking, because a lot of people think fishing's a bamboo pole and a six pack of beer. But it's a bit rougher than that. Would you say you're a morning person?"

"I start livin' after midnight, man," Sandy replied, trying to sound mature.

"Good. 'Cause that's about when you'll be getting up tomorrow. How about seasickness?"

"I can handle it."

Porter laughed. " 'Course you can," he said. " 'Course you can."

❀❀❀

The sea was rough when they went out at dawn. It tossed the boat relentlessly, drenching Sandy from head to toe. But Porter didn't seem to notice. He steered the boat without saying a word. When he finally turned off the motor, he still didn't speak. He just sat back and took in the open sea. Once in a while he smiled, as if he had discovered a private thought.

"I love it out here," Porter said with a long sigh. "It's perfect in every way." Then he readied his pole without saying another word, while the boat bobbed and heaved in the waves. "Where's that bait?" he called out to Sandy.

Sandy carried the two heavy pails to his uncle and tried to steady himself. He was determined not to let Porter see how sick he was. But it was difficult. The smell of the fish was making his stomach turn over and over and over.

Sandy tried, but it was no use. His stomach won, and he fell to his knees and retched his guts out over the side of the boat.

"You OK?" Porter asked, when Sandy seemed to have finished throwing up everything but his intestines.

"I'll . . . live," Sandy managed to mutter. But he didn't really believe it. Not for a minute.

☼☼☼

A sleek party boat took his mind off his stomach. The words *Bounty Hunter* adorned its hull. Weekenders intent on partying lined its decks. Sandy could tell that they were laughing at Porter's pathetic old trawler, and for some reason that annoyed him. He wasn't sure why he should care about anything having to do with Porter.

"Hey! It floats!" a man on the party boat hollered. He was leaning on the railing and grinning down at them. There was something really creepy about him. Something mean.

"Shut up, Moran," Porter called back.

"Who's that?" Sandy asked Porter when the man had moved away from the railing.

"He owns that boat, and I'd suggest you stay away from him. He's everything you do not want to be in life."

The weekenders were dropping their fishing lines now. They were

moving their chairs to the railing, settling in with their beers.

Suddenly, one of them stood and raised his pole. He had something. But then he hesitated and called to the skipper. "Hey Dirk!" he whined. "A damn dolphin stole my fish! That wasn't in the brochure!"

"They're scaring the fish away, Moran!" another one shouted. "What am I paying for here?"

Sandy listened, then turned just in time to see several dolphins leap out of the water. More followed, rising into the air like dancers. Sandy's breath caught in his throat as he watched them. He had never seen anything like this before. It was an amazing sight.

"Great, eh?" Porter said, watching him. "Almost enough to take your mind off your stomach."

"Well, almost," Sandy admitted.

As he said it, a gunshot rang out over the ocean. Another followed. Then another, and another. The next time Sandy looked, the dolphins had disappeared into the sea. Sandy glanced up at the deck of the Bounty Hunter. Dirk Moran was dusting off his gun.

"Yeah!" Sandy called. "Way to fish!"

Instantly, Porter was beside him. His eyes were filled with fire. Anger was making his whole body tremble. "What did you say?" he hissed at Sandy.

"I don't—"

Porter's eyes silenced Sandy before he could think of a retort. His uncle leaned closer so that Sandy would be sure to hear what he had to say. "That's not fishing, kid. That's murder. And it's pathetic."

Chapter 3

Not far from Dirk Moran's *Bounty Hunter*, a small dolphin was looking for his mother. The little dolphin moved through the dark water until he found her. Her large body was sinking slowly. He swam to her, nudged her upward, freed her blowhole, and waited. She breathed for a moment. But she was too badly injured to survive. After a while he had to let her go.

The skipper of the *Bounty Hunter* shot at the young dolphin again, sending him underwater. And when he was gone, he shot again, and again, until the hunter, too, was sure the mother dolphin was dead.

Sandy saw it all. He moved to the side of the boat and gazed into the sea. He studied the water carefully, but there was no sign of the little dolphin. For some reason, he felt sad. But that was silly. It was only a fish, wasn't it?

A splashing sound shook him, and he wheeled around. The young dolphin was there, behind him, bobbing in the water.

Sandy ran to the other side of the boat and looked down. But Dirk Moran's voice brought him back.

"Hey, you!" Moran hollered.

Sandy turned and glanced up at the party boat.

"You see that other dolphin?" Dirk called.

Sandy hesitated, then pointed in the wrong direction. "He went that way," he called back.

When the *Bounty Hunter* was gone, Sandy grinned and returned to the little dolphin. "You'd better get out of here," he said. But the dolphin didn't move. He blinked up at Sandy with soft, gentle eyes.

"Go!" Sandy ordered.

The dolphin rose up out of the water. Then he dove down and was gone.

❀ ❀ ❀

Sandy didn't speak as Porter brought the trawler in and tied it up. He was thinking about the dolphin, and the men who had shot its mother. He was trying to sort out everything he had seen. Porter, this guy Moran, and the weekenders who only cared about having a good time.

When the boat was secure, Porter went into the store. Sandy watched him go. Then he rushed over to the phone booth to call Joel.

"How is it?" Joel asked.

"It's heaven—if you like getting up at five in the morning to get sick on an old dump of a boat. And it's great, if you like watching drunken weekenders shoot a bunch of dolphins!"

"Does that mean we're still on for the concert?" Joel asked.

"I wouldn't miss it for anything. I'll be there if it's the last thing I ever do!" Sandy promised. "But I've gotta go. The hippie's back, and he's looking for me."

He hung up and followed Porter over to a small weathered building. A sign in front read BAIT & TACKLE SHACK. Sandy could see that Porter was still upset about what had happened to the dolphins.

"Sorry you had to see that out there," Porter said as they approached the door. "Moran's no fisherman. He's got no respect for the sea. Sure, dolphins can be a nuisance. They eat your bait and tear up your nets. But they were out there first."

"Isn't it against the law to shoot them?" Sandy asked.

"Especially in my water," Porter replied angrily.

Sandy hesitated and thought about that one. "Didn't know you could own the water," he said.

"I've been fishing that spot for years, and everybody knows it's my spot. OK, so I don't own it. Maybe you could say I sort of have a lease on the area. But no matter how you see it, nobody should be shooting at anything out there."

Porter stomped over to a little work bench on the porch. A small person in a hooded parka and galoshes was sitting there. He was surrounded by so much electronic paraphernalia that Sandy could hardly see him.

"Yo," Porter said. "It's the Marvelous One."

The little person didn't move, or speak.

"You a little warm in there, Marv?" Porter asked.

Marvin glanced up. But again he said nothing. He picked up a blow torch and turned back to his work.

Sandy and Porter turned away. "What's wrong with him?" Sandy asked.

"He's a little shy. But give him a spring and a piece of wire," replied Porter, the admiration clear in his voice, "and he'll give you an outboard motor."

They went inside and looked around. Porter wanted to talk to the woman behind the counter, but she was busy.

"I won't be long," she said, as she helped a little girl thread a worm onto a fishhook.

"But I don't want to hurt him," the little girl was saying. "Look! He's alive. He's wiggling."

The woman took the worm from the hook and put it back with his friends. "All right," she said. "Then let's use this guy." She held up a rubber worm and smiled.

When the girl was gone, the woman joined them on the other

side of the store. "You must be Sandy," she said. "We've all been waiting to meet you. I'm Cathy."

"Cathy's a marine biologist," Porter explained. "She knows everything there is to know about the sea. If you have any questions, she's the one to ask."

Sandy shrugged and shook her hand. Then he stepped back and checked out the spear guns.

"I'm glad you came in," Cathy said to Porter. "You know those dead fish you brought me last week? I just got the lab tests back. They were loaded with Dioxin."

"Dioxin?" Porter said.

"It's a byproduct of herbicides," Cathy replied gravely. "Herbicides are weed killers, Porter. Poison. Really nasty stuff. It can kill fish faster than anything around—which may also explain why your take of fish has gone down lately."

"Yeah, maybe," Porter said thoughtfully. "But how'd Dioxin get into our water in the first place? Somebody dumping?"

Cathy shook her head and frowned. "Got me," she said. "Maybe it's a mistake. They're running more tests."

Cathy walked over to the window and glanced out. "Careful Marvin," she called. "Watch it with that thing."

But Marvin didn't look up. His head was bent over his work. He was concentrating on his blowtorch. Marvin had a serious crush on Cathy, but he also knew that since he was just a kid, the only excuse he had for hanging out with her all the time was to be making and fixing things around the shack where she spent a lot of time. Marvelous Marvin loved fixing things, so he was happy as a clam.

Cathy turned from Marvin back to Porter and grinned. "Think we'll ever get him out of that smelly parka, Porter?"

"Maybe we could dry clean it with him inside," Porter suggested. "I can't think of any other way."

Cathy shoved him and laughed. "So, by the way, when are we

getting married?"

So that's how it is, Sandy thought. He suddenly remembered that Cathy was the same woman he'd seen pulling the boat. Sandy waited for his uncle's answer. Somehow he knew what it would be.

"Uh, well, uh . . . I just remembered!" Porter said triumphantly. "I have a roast in the oven. And I really should press my suit. And my library book's overdue. I've gotta go now."

Predictable, Sandy thought. That man is nothing if not predictable.

Porter was backing out the door. The excuses just kept coming. As he passed Sandy, he yanked ahold of his shirt and dragged him out with him. Then they walked back to the trawler together and headed home.

"I'm going out for dinner," Porter announced after they had showered and were settled in. "I'll be at Cathy's. Here's the number. You know where the food is."

"SpaghettiOs," Sandy groaned.

"Right!" he said with a grin. "And I'm afraid the TV only gets weather channels."

"My favorite. I'm gonna hit the hay early."

"Good thinking. Well, I'll see you in the A.M., kid."

✸ ✸ ✸

The music from the clock radio blasted Porter awake at 5:00 the next morning. When the song ended, the announcer gave the weather report. A tropical storm was gaining strength. Porter groaned. Just what he needed. A bad storm could take the place apart once and for all.

He crawled out of bed as he always did, slowly, and plopped some SpaghettiOs into a pan.

"Move it, kid!" he shouted when the food was ready. "I'm not kidding. There's a great meal brewing out here in this fine kitchen. Come and get it."

No answer. Porter dropped the spoon and peeked into the back room. The lump under the blanket wasn't stirring.

"It's morning, buddy!" Porter said. "It's time to go to get started. Fish await us. How about it?"

Still no answer. Porter moved closer and grabbed the end of the blanket. "Hate to do this, kid. But iiiiit's showtime!"

He yanked the blanket away. But nothing was there. Except for a couple of pillows, the bed was empty. Sandy was gone.

Chapter 4

The sky was beginning to darken as Sandy boarded the ferry. A strong gust of wind tossed him into a seat by the window. He was free. By tonight, he'd be backstage at the Red Hot Chili Peppers concert, and he'd never have to go fishing again.

Sandy was so busy thinking about the concert that he didn't hear Porter's trawler angle up through the waves to the side of the larger vessel. He wasn't even aware that the ferry had stopped. He didn't see Porter climb onto the ferry. And he didn't hear his footsteps coming toward him.

Then, suddenly, there Uncle Porter was, standing right smack in front of him.

Sandy jumped to his feet and raced to the other side of the ferry. But Porter was too fast for him. Porter snatched him by the lapel and dragged him down the aisle.

"Get off me, you psycho!" Sandy shouted as he struggled to get rid of his uncle.

But it was no use. Within minutes, they were on their way back to the island. Gale-force winds plummeted them as they approached the dock. The gusts stirred up the water and shook the trawler. But Sandy was too angry to care. All he wanted was to get away from his uncle.

"Get the rope!" Porter hollered as the boat heaved and crashed against the dock. Porter grabbed a piling and hung on.

But Sandy wasn't listening. He had to get out of there—and fast. The second the boat was close enough to the dock, he stumbled over the railing and was gone. He raced across the lawn, but there was nowhere to go. The wind was raging now. It was pulling at him and moving him sideways. The gale was so strong Sandy felt as if it would lift him up and carry him away like a feather.

"Sandy, stop!" Porter called. "It's too dangerous!"

But Sandy didn't stop. He fought the wind as best he could until someone's arms brought him down. It was Porter. His uncle was tackling him. He was carrying him through the grass, toward the house, and then, unbelievably, he was shoving him into the cellar.

"Great!" Porter groaned, when they were safely inside. "Instead of chasing you I could have been boarding up my windows. This is going to be some wicked storm!"

But Sandy didn't care. He didn't care if the storm destroyed the place. He folded his arms and looked around the cellar. It seemed fitting. Not only was he not on his way to the concert. He was stuck in a cellar filled with candles and canned food.

"Do you know what you just did?" Sandy shouted. "Do you have any idea? This was going to be the most important night of my life, man!"

"I certainly *do* know what I did!" Porter shouted back. "I saved your life. And the way I feel right now I'll unfortunately just have to live with that fact!"

"You made me blow laminates to Red Hot Chili Peppers. Now what do I do?" Sandy fumed. "The next concert's in Orlando, and I don't have tickets, or money!"

Just then the power went out and the lights fluttered off, leaving them in total darkness.

"Oh, great!" Porter sighed. "This is just great!" He staggered around in the dark rummaging around for a candle which he proceeded to light. "What was it that I said to your parents when they asked me to take you for the summer? Something like, 'Love to see Sandy. Send him down. It'll cost my house and boat. But that's OK. Anything for family. No problem at all.' " Porter stared at Sandy stonefaced.

"Then why didn't you just let me go?" Sandy demanded.

Porter sighed and shook his head. "Because I'm not done with you. Does that answer your question?"

Porter glared at Sandy who glared right back. While the storm howled and whistled outside, they did not speak. Eventually, they managed to fall asleep. When they awoke it was morning—and Porter's world was in splinters.

The wind had ripped the screens off the house. Gutters sagged. Trees lay broken on the ground. But the worst disaster of all was the trawler. The boat was smashed and completely filled with water. Only Pete seemed happy about the boat's new use. He was using it as his own private swimming pool.

Porter closed his eyes, then opened them again and sighed. "Look," he said to Sandy who was staring around in disbelief. "Since I know how in love you are with being here, I'll make you a deal. You help me get this mess cleaned up, and I'll make sure you get to that concert in Orlando."

Sandy was stunned. What was the catch? "How? I don't even have tickets anymore."

"You're dealing with Porter Ricks, kid. If it exists, I'll get it. We'll make that show."

Aha, the catch. "We?" Sandy asked incredulously.

"You don't think I'd let you go alone, do you?" Porter smiled and offered his hand in a truce. Sandy hesitated. But then he shook it because he wanted to go to that concert so badly he could taste it. And maybe, just maybe, his uncle would come through.

The tug arrived that afternoon and towed the wrecked trawler away, with Porter up to his knees in water inside it. "I'm leaving you here," Porter said before he left. "Start with the fish-pen netting. There are masks and things in the shed. Anything else you need you can get in town."

"How deep is it?" Sandy glanced down. The pen seemed to be carved out of coral, and he could not see the bottom.

"Not very. Don't you swim?"

When Sandy muttered, "Of course!" Porter wasn't entirely convinced.

"It's barely five feet," Porter added. "If you get nervous, just stand up. I might be gone for a few days. I gotta stay with the boat. Will you be OK?"

"Yeah . . ." But this time it was Sandy who wasn't so sure. The thought of SpaghettiOs for breakfast, lunch, and dinner in the house that was even more wrecked than it had been before was not exactly appetizing.

When Porter was gone, Sandy found a mask, a snorkel, and a very large life preserver in the shed. He put them on and dropped into the fish pen.

He touched the bottom, found solid ground, and stood. It was all right down there. He reached out, awakening a small starfish which was resting on the edge of the coral reef. Sponges, barnacles, and small bright fish glided through the water about him. He turned and brushed against a patch of brilliant red coral. He leaned over to study it more carefully, and—what!—?

A dolphin was in Sandy's face. Right there in front of his mask. It was staring right at him.

Sandy did the only normal thing to do: He panicked. Flailing his arms and yelling through his snorkel, he stumbled toward the shore. Safe at last on dry land, he turned to face the beast. The dolphin was at least fifteen feet in the air. When it came down it splashed onto

its side. Then it bobbed back up and let out a "Yip!" It was showing off for him!

Sandy caught his breath and then felt a little foolish for overreacting. "Are you trying to give me a heart attack?" he shouted.

The dolphin tail-walked across the water. Then it flipped over and nodded happily.

"Think that's funny? Go away!" Sandy said. "I'm going into town. You better be gone when I get back here."

Sandy fished Porter's old bike from the shed and rode into town, going straight to the General Store. He ordered a tuna sub. When it was ready, he carried it to the town dock and settled down to eat it. After the ferocious storm the night before, the day was strangely pleasant and calm. The ferry was out and no one was around. For some reason, Sandy decided he liked the silence.

A girl came and sat nearby on the dock. After she had been there for a while, she pulled a mouth harp out of her pocket and began to play it. For some reason, neither her presence nor the strange music bothered Sandy. She looked liked she was about his age. He watched her and noticed that she was playing to something or someone in the water. He moved closer and looked down. The little dolphin was there, watching her.

"Like my dolphin?" Sandy asked, moving even closer.

"*Your* dolphin?"

"That's right," Sandy said. "I found him."

"What's his name?"

Sandy was stumped on that one. He watched the little dolphin for several moments, thinking. Then it raised a flipper as if to wave hello. "Flipper," he answered.

"I've never seen one alone like this," the girl said. "They're usually with their families. They're not much good without their families. And I'll tell you one thing. Alone, he'd be no match for Scar."

"Who's Scar?" Sandy asked.

"The hammerhead shark that stalks these waters. Big and ugly. Legend has it he took out a boat full of tourists. But I don't believe it," she grinned. "So, if he's really yours, make him do something!"

Sandy had to think about that one. After a while, he held a piece of his tuna sub over the water and waited.

Flipper came through. He rose up, snatched the sandwich, and disappeared.

"Cool!" the girl said and laughed. "By the way, I'm Kim."

"Sandy."

Suddenly Flipper emerged, took one look at Sandy's sandwich and whined.

"Hey, he's hungry," Kim said.

"He can get his own fish."

Kim turned to Sandy and shook her head. "Maybe he can't," she said. "Fishing's not that great these days. And dolphins eat fifteen pounds a day. That's how they get their water. They're mammals, you know. They breathe air just like us. If their blowholes aren't above the water, then they can't breathe."

"How do you know so much?" Sandy asked.

"When you're surrounded by water, you get pretty familiar with it. Besides, I'm going to be a marine biologist like Cathy at the bait shop. So where are you going to get the fish to feed your dolphin, Mr. Big Shot?"

When he didn't answer, Kim led him over to a boat filled with fish. "Don't tell them what you need it for," she whispered. "People around here don't like dolphins."

Kim approached an old fisherman and smiled a dazzling smile. "Hi, Mr. Dunnahy," she said. "This is my friend, Sandy. He's visiting and needs fish, you know, for bait and chum. Maybe you need some work done?"

The old man looked him over. "Can you scrub a deck?"

"Scrub a deck?" Sandy repeated, appalled.

Kim moved closer and gave him a nudge. He flashed the old man a smile and said, "Sure. No problem."

An hour later they were back at the end of the dock. There was a pail of fish between them, and Flipper was waiting. They tossed the fish to the little dolphin one at a time. And every time Flipper caught one, the young dolphin seemed to grow a little bit stronger.

"Think I could come by and see Flipper some time?" Kim asked as Sandy rose to leave. The pail was empty. It was time to go home. "I don't have a lot of friends. I guess I'm just too mature for my age."

"Sure," said Sandy. He didn't think Kim was all that bad—for a girl. "I don't know too many girls who'd stick their hands in a bucket of dead fish."

Kim left, but Flipper wouldn't go away. As Sandy rode home along the shore road, the dolphin followed him in the water. When Sandy dodged behind bushes or houses to hide from him, Flipper watched him and chattered. When Sandy sped up, Flipper sped up, too. Flipper stayed nearby as Sandy repaired the nets. He was there when Sandy hammered an old tire back onto the dock. The dolphin was like some kind of a weird magnet that wouldn't let go.

"Will you get lost already?" Sandy shouted.

But Flipper didn't. Instead, he flipped an old watch onto the dock and waited for Sandy's reaction.

Sandy was impressed. "Very nice," he called. "Now go find something else."

Flipper dove under the surface of the water. He emerged a minute later and tossed a half dollar into the air.

"Dude!" Sandy shouted, as he caught it in mid-air. Suddenly an idea struck him. This fish might be a walking, swimming, dancing money magnet. If he had to stay on that island, then he might as well start a business.

"I've got a great idea," he said to Flipper. "You need fish, and I could always use some cash. We could make a great team. What do

you say we go into business together?"

When Flipper yipped, Sandy grinned. Maybe this was it. Maybe this would be his real new beginning.

Chapter 5

When Porter's pickup pulled into the driveway a few days later, Sandy's new business was already in full swing.

DIVING FOR DOLLARS read one of the signs. Another read: TOSS A QUARTER! FLIPPER RETURNS!

Sandy was delighted. Flipper had learned his job well. Every time a child tossed him a coin, Flipper caught it and dropped it into a pail in the sand. Then he plucked a penny from another pail and gave it to the child. This dolphin was brilliant! In fact, this dolphin was a genius!

Kim didn't recognize Porter. She stepped up to the truck and smiled sweetly. "Sir," she said. "I'm afraid I can't let you in without a fish. Everyone needs a fish to get into this party."

Porter glared at her. "You've got to be kidding! I don't need anything to get in, kid! This is my house!" He glanced around the yard and groaned. None of the repair or cleanup work had been done after the storm. Nothing! He slammed the truck into first gear and drove to the dock.

Sandy was waiting for him. And the second he glanced at his uncle's face, he could see he was in big trouble.

"What's going on?" Porter hissed.

"Oh, hi. It's the Flipper show."

At the sound of his name, Flipper rose out of the water and bowed.

Porter took it all in and understood in a second what was going on. "Time to go home!," he announced to the crowd. "The show's over!"

Terrified of the furious adult, the kids left quickly. When they were gone, Porter confronted Sandy. "Didn't we have a deal?" he shouted. "Something about working on the house?"

"I did it so Flipper could eat," he whined.

But Sandy wasn't fooling Porter. "Who do you think you're dealing with, you little half-pint thief? You did it to turn some coin! All right, we're going to try a whole new approach. This is how it works."

Sandy stiffened and stared at the ground.

"One! You will learn to take responsibility for your actions. Two! You will get up for work on time, and you will not complain. Three! You will take care of that dolphin now that it won't leave. And four! You will hand over all profits from your sweet little business!"

Sandy hesitated. But he could see that Porter meant business, so he handed over the quarters. Then he folded his arms and glared as Porter stomped away.

That afternoon Sandy scrubbed a deck in return for a pail of fish. And the next morning Flipper got breakfast.

There seemed to be no bottom to Flipper's appetite. He caught the fish in mid-air. He grabbed for them, flipped for them, walked backward for them, and flashed, nodded, and danced for them.

Pelican Pete watched them from a dock post. He looked hungry, but Sandy wasn't wasting any fish on him. He got plenty to eat on his own. Instead, he tossed yet another fish to Flipper. Flipper rose up and caught the fish. But this time he didn't swallow it. He held it in his mouth, then flipped it over to Pete with his snout.

Pete chomped it down and squawked happily.

When the pail was empty, Flipper yipped and jumped. He seemed to be asking Sandy to come in and play.

"Forget about it," Sandy laughed, rising to leave. "You're surf, and I'm turf." He leaned over and started to pick up the pail, but he did not make it. A swift slap on his bottom sent him flailing into the water.

"Whoa!" Sandy spluttered once he had surfaced. He tried to climb back up onto the dock, but Flipper was too quick for him. Flipper dove right at him and brought him back into the water.

"So, you want to play, do you?" Sandy said, turning onto his back. Flipper did the same. The dolphin's backstroke was almost perfect.

Sandy flipped over and stood on his hands. Flipper stood on his head.

Sandy grabbed Flipper's dorsal fin. Flipper yipped and set off. Sandy could not believe it. There he was, hitching a high-speed ride from a dolphin! This was totally cool! Clutching the fin, Sandy and Flipper cut through the water. Together they charged through the cove, like a rider and a stallion.

They played until sunset, then rested in the fish pen until the sun had disappeared entirely. When it was almost dark, Sandy glanced behind him. A small figure was standing there. It was Marvin. He was watching them. Sandy smiled and waved, but Marvin just stood still.

※ ◎ ※

"What would you be doing right now if you were back in Chicago?" Kim asked the next day. They were riding their bikes along the shore road. Another pail of fish was hanging from Sandy's handlebars.

"I don't know. Maybe I'd be hanging out at the mall."

"I've never been to a mall," Kim said. "Uh, when are you leaving?"

"Couple of weeks. Soon as my parents get back from Europe. Why?"

"Well, last year I skipped a grade. And I was just thinking, like, if you stayed and lived with your uncle, we could be in the same class."

Sandy smiled and glanced over at her. He liked her. She was . . .

"SANDY!" Kim shouted. "WATCH OUT!"

He looked up just in time to see the battered pickup truck

screeching to a stop. Sandy swerved and wiped out. The fish went everywhere.

It took him a moment to realize that he was alive. He stood carefully, brushing the fish aside, and faced the driver. It was Dirk Moran, the skipper of the *Bounty Hunter*.

"You'd better be careful on that bike," Moran smirked. "If you don't watch where you're going, you might get hurt."

When Sandy didn't answer, Moran gunned his truck and steered it into the parking lot of the nearest seedy bar.

That evening, Sandy decided not to mention the incident to Porter. There was no point. Dirk Moran was a jerk, and Sandy could handle him if he had to.

Sandy and Kim took the fish home, gave them to Flipper, and went to work. Sandy concentrated on retying the torn netting. Kim noticed something else. Hiding behind a tree, watching them, was Marvin. "Sandy," Kim whispered. "Look."

Sandy turned and followed Kim's gaze. When he saw Marvin there in his parka, he smiled. "Hey, Marv," he called. "What's up?"

Marvin didn't answer, so Sandy climbed out of the pen and walked toward him. He turned and stood beside him.

"Pretty cool, huh?" Sandy laughed. Flipper and Kim were splashing around in the pen below them.

Marvin again didn't respond in any way.

"Wanna pet him?"

This time Marvin smiled. And then he ran. He raced down to the dock and skidded to a stop at the end. Without missing a beat, he dropped his parka, his heavy undershirt, and his galoshes. He ripped off his socks and his pants and simply stood there, shivering in his boxer shorts. Flipper floated over to him and looked up. They stared at each other for a long time—then Marvin cannonballed into the water.

"You all right, Marvin?" Sandy asked when the kid came up coughing. But Marvin wasn't interested in Sandy. His eyes were on

FLIPPER THE
WONDER DOLPHIN!
ADMISSION $1.00

AND A FISH

DRINKS
$1.50

DONATIONS
FOR FLIPPERS FUND

Flipper. Flipper was moving closer, and Marvin looked nervous.

"It's OK," Sandy said. "Let him come to you."

Flipper floated even closer and brushed up against Marvin. Marvin grinned and held out his hand to the little dolphin. He was running his fingers over Flipper's body when Cathy and Porter pulled up.

Cathy saw Marvin and gasped. She had been looking for him everywhere. While not in school, Marvin had never left the bait shop on his own before, and she had been terrified. And now here the kid was, in the water with a dolphin. And he was laughing!

She raced to the water's edge and looked down. "Honey?" she said.

Marvin turned and looked up. And then he did something that he had never done in his life. Marvin spoke. "Flipper!" he said.

Cathy's eyes filled with tears. She looked at Sandy and Flipper, Porter and Kim, and finally at Marvin.

As Porter's arm slipped around her, she smiled and whispered, "Yeah, Flipper."

Chapter 6

The next time Sandy saw Dirk Moran was in a restaurant in town called The Barnacle. Sandy was sitting at a table with Porter, Cathy, Kim, and Marvin when Moran approached them.

"Word's out you got a pet dolphin, Ricks," Moran muttered. He spread his hands out on the table and leaned down toward Porter.

"I wouldn't call him a pet." Porter did not look up. He was flexing and fisting his hands on the table.

Dirk picked up an empty glass and started polishing it absent-mindedly. "With fishing the way it's been lately, we sure don't need dolphins tearing nets," he said. "Don't need them stealing bait and causing regulations. But you know all that."

"We're talking about one dolphin, Dirk," Cathy reminded him. "One very small dolphin, in fact."

Dirk narrowed his eyes. "Stay out of it, Miss Heal-the-Bay. One dolphin's one too many. If you don't take care of it, somebody else will." He turned and stomped out of the restaurant. That was a threat if Sandy had ever heard one. And he was sure that little warning was not Dirk Moran's last word on the subject of Flipper.

They all took their time eating then strolled down to the town dock. A crowd seemed to be gathering near the ferry.

"What's the guy's problem, anyway?" Sandy asked Porter when they were almost there.

"Dirk Moran resents any life form more intelligent than he is. And that pretty much covers everything, including . . ." Porter hesitated. Hoots were rising out of the crowd on the dock. Some men were hollering and laughing about something.

Sandy walked faster toward the crowd and stopped behind a group of fishermen. "What's going on?" he asked.

"We snagged this guy hanging around the dock. He won't try *that* again!" The fisherman pointed to the water and laughed.

Sandy pushed closer to the edge and looked down into the water. It was Flipper, and he was going crazy. The fishermen had tied a rope around his tail. They were pulling the other end, as if it were a game of tug-of-war. And they were winning.

"Hoo-ee!" the men called. "Ride 'em!"

"What are you doing?" Sandy shouted. "Cut it out! You're hurting him!"

"He's a bait snatcher!" someone hollered.

Sandy pushed closer and tried to grab the rope, But it was no use. The crowd was closing in. He was outnumbered.

"Lookee, Dirk! We've got a live one!" somebody shouted as they grabbed Sandy and held him tight.

Dirk Moran stepped up and grinned. "Hello again!" he said with a triumphant grin. "Is there something we can do for you?"

"Lemme go! Stop!" Sandy tried to wiggle away. But they pinned his arms until he couldn't move. They yanked the rope harder. Sandy pleaded with them, but they wouldn't stop.

"Enough!" Porter finally yelled. "You've had your fun. Can't you see the animal means something to the kid? Now leave him alone!" The fishermen let Sandy go. But Flipper was still trapped and no one had made a move to free the poor animal. Porter snapped open his buck knife and cut the rope. The rope slipped into the water, and

Flipper swam away.

Porter then spun around and faced the crowd. "I mean it now!" he announced fiercely. "I said enough! If I ever see another display like that again I'll—"

Dirk stepped up to Porter. "You got no right doing that, Ricks," he hissed. "That dolphin's a menace! I oughta teach you a lesson right now!"

"I'd like that, Moran," Porter warned, moving closer to Dirk. "I have a thirst for knowledge."

The two men stood frozen, eyes locked, for several moments. Sandy watched them in fear. He didn't doubt that Porter could take on Moran, but what about an entire dock full of cruel idiots? They were outnumbered. Suddenly Porter whirled around. He knew Moran was not worth the effort. Sandy breathed a sigh of relief.

It took several days to get Flipper back to normal. It was Cathy who accomplished it. She stayed with him while Sandy and Porter worked on the house. Hour after hour, she massaged his bruised tail and calmed the poor dolphin.

Porter was putting up fence slats when he heard the boat. When he saw that it was the U.S. MARINE AND FISHERIES vessel, he was delighted. He hadn't seen Buck Cowen in months. He dropped his hammer and wandered down to the water. When the boat docked, he shook Buck's hand.

"Haven't seen you in ages, Buck," Porter said. "It's been way too long. How you been?"

"Just fine, Porter. You?"

"Bit of storm damage. Nothing terrible. What's up?"

"Well, a little birdie told me you folks found yourselves this animal." Buck nodded toward Flipper. But he kept his eye on Porter. "You can't keep a dolphin, Porter. We got a thing called the Marine Mammal Protection Act that Congress takes pretty seriously. You know that."

"We don't keep him, Buck," Porter said. "He just stays. Guess he likes it around here. But who wouldn't?"

"It doesn't really matter, Porter. The law says that animal has to be in a licensed captivity program. Either that, or he has to be at sea. And they don't take that law lightly," Buck explained. "But you know that."

Porter stepped back and looked over Buck's shoulder. The crew on Buck's vessel seemed to be waiting for something.

"Buck, are you here to take him away?" Porter asked.

But Buck didn't answer. He just stared at his boots.

"You can't do that!" Sandy cried. "He can't survive on his own. He's used to being fed."

"Sandy's right," Cathy agreed. "The animal's mother was shot. Flipper probably can't fend for himself anymore."

Buck glanced up at them, his eyes pleading. "Don't make it hard on me," he said. "They'll just go stick him in some aquarium and revoke your fishing license. It's a clear-cut situation. I don't have any choice, Porter. So let's do this in a friendly way. I could use your help."

Porter and Cathy looked at one another. Without exchanging a word, they both knew that they could not fight the law. So they sighed and set to work.

But Sandy couldn't watch. As Porter and Buck's crew hoisted Flipper onto a canvas stretcher, he wandered up to the house and plopped despondently into the hammock. He turned on the radio and pumped it up till it blasted. He didn't want to hear. He didn't want to know.

When they were finished, Porter came inside and flipped off the radio. "You want to come or you going to stay here?" he asked gently.

Sandy didn't answer. He pretended to not even hear.

"All set?" Buck called.

Porter turned and headed back out to the boat. It took Sandy a few seconds before he realized that if he didn't go, he'd never get a

chance to say goodbye to Flipper. He heaved himself off the hammock and raced out behind his uncle.

Sandy sat beside Flipper as they moved slowly out to sea. He stroked him and poured water over his frightened body.

"It'll be all right," Sandy said, trying to convince himself as well as Flipper. "It will be all right."

But it wasn't all right. When the boat reached the open sea, they lowered him over the side. But Flipper didn't go away. He just stayed there, beside the boat, and watched them. Then he yipped, and rose up, and Sandy knew he wanted to play. Sandy wanted to jump into the water and go to him. He wanted to hold his tail and be pulled through the water. But he knew he couldn't do that. So he just left him there and went into the ship's cabin.

As the boat started up, he heard Flipper's final yip. Then the boat's motor was gunned and it moved away from the puzzled dolphin.

There was nothing at all that Sandy could do about it. Nothing.

Chapter 7

Sandy?" Kim called softly. It was later that night, much later, and they were both out on the dock.

Sandy knelt down on the dock and grasped the side of the little dinghy. Then he pulled it closer and climbed in. "This thing doesn't look too steady," he whispered.

"It's fine. Quick, get in!"

When Sandy was settled, Kim pulled the cord on the motor. In a minute they were on their way. It took them a long time to get back to where they had left Flipper, and even then they weren't sure it was the right spot. They cut the engine and listened.

"Flipper!" Sandy called. "Flipper! Flipper?"

But there was no answer, except for the sound of the wind and the sea. Kim found the oars and rowed gently, calling his name, but there was still no answer.

They called for half an hour before they noticed the boat. It was huge. And it was coming straight toward them!

They didn't know whether to scream or start the motor and gun it out of there. As the boat slowly got closer, they were able to make out the shadows of several men. The men were standing near the railing. And they were dumping something over the side.

"What is it?" Kim whispered.

"Looks like some kind of barrels."

The men were pointing now. They were signaling and calling to each other. Sandy slid down and peered into the darkness. "Are they pointing at us?" he whispered.

"I don't know," Kim said. "But let's get out of here."

Sandy wrapped the pull-cord around the outboard and yanked. But it was an old rope, and it didn't hold. The rope frayed, then snapped, then ripped right out of its casing.

They were trapped. The boat was even closer now. It was almost on top of them. Kim scrambled to the oars and rowed, as fast as she could, until they were out of the way. She rowed frantically, keeping her eyes on the boat. The men weren't looking at them anymore.

"Maybe they didn't see us," Sandy whispered. "Maybe they were pointing at something else."

As Kim rowed for home, Sandy glanced back at the boat. It was familiar. He had seen it before. And then he saw the name on the hull. It was the *Bounty Hunter*. Just what was Dirk Moran up to?

◈ ◈ ◈

Sandy slept in the hammock that night. And the next morning he didn't mention his late night travels at sea—nor what he and Kim had witnessed. He knew that Porter wouldn't be happy that he'd been out at night in the first place.

Porter must have noticed Sandy's mood. "I know you miss him," he said. "But he belongs out there."

"Seems like things always mess up once you start caring about them," Sandy muttered.

"It's good you cared about Flipper, Sandy," Porter told him. "People who don't care wind up in a home drooling creamed spinach."

"You sound like my mom."

"Your mother cares about you," Porter said.

But Sandy wasn't so sure about that. "Then why did she dump

me here?" he asked. "My whole summer was planned!"

"It wasn't such a bad move," Porter replied. "Flipper's alive because of you. He'd be dead now if you hadn't been around."

"OK. So tell me why my mother's in my face all the time? Nothing I do is ever good enough for her."

Porter had to think about that one for a while. After a moment, he said, "Maybe she knows she doesn't have much time before you're on your own. Maybe she just wants the best for you. Sometimes that makes moms act like jerks."

Porter came over to the hammock and rustled Sandy's hair. And then he remembered something. He pulled a small ticket envelope out of his back pocket and handed it to Sandy. Sandy turned it over a couple of times and then he looked up at his uncle and grinned.

"Is this what I think it is?"

"Front and center seats to Red Hot Chili Peppers," Porter said proudly. "You and me, my friend."

"You're really going with me?"

"Why not?"

Sandy shrugged and grinned again. Red Hot Chili Peppers! Wicked cool! Sandy was trying to think of what to say next when Kim rode up on her bike. She was tromping up the porch steps when Pete the Pelican started squawking his head off.

"What's the matter. Pete?" she asked.

Pete hesitated then raced toward the dock. Kim followed and looked down into the water. "Sandy!" she called.

Within seconds, Sandy was beside her. Below them, gazing up with pain-filled eyes, was Flipper! His bruised and terrified little body bobbed below them. He was sinking.

Sandy leapt into the water and held him up so that he could breathe. Kim jumped in to help him.

"Do something, Sandy!" she cried.

"Just hold him! Don't let him sink!"

While Kim held him, Sandy ran back into the house. He grabbed the hammock off its rings. Then he ran back to the dock where he fashioned a makeshift sling. He nailed one end to the dock and the other to some slats that he had pounded into the soft sand.

Then, gently, Sandy and Kim rolled the little dolphin onto the sling. They turned him on his side, then on his stomach. When his blowhole could bring in air, they ran their fingers over his shivering body.

"Stay with him," Sandy said. "He's scared. Don't leave him—no matter what!" Then he jumped onto his bike. This time Sandy pumped, pushing faster than he had ever pushed in his life. He gunned the pedals with a force he didn't believe possible. And when he reached Cathy's Bait & Tackle Shack, he didn't stop. He dropped the bike and raced up the steps.

Cathy was helping a fisherman count boxes. Standing beside her, wearing only boxers and a welder's flip hat, was Marvin. Sandy couldn't help but blink—Marvin's boxer shorts were so bright they were practically blinding.

"You gotta come quick!" Sandy shouted.

Cathy turned toward him and frowned. "What's wrong?"

"I think Flipper's dying."

Cathy didn't hesitate. Within minutes, Cathy, Sandy, and Marvin were racing back to Porter's in her convertible. Kim was waiting for them. She was still next to Flipper. As Cathy examined him, Kim stood beside Sandy and waited .

"He's dehydrated," Cathy muttered. She opened Flipper's mouth and studied his tongue. "Something's wrong. Hard to tell. Maybe something he's eaten. I'll do some tests."

She glanced up. Porter's trawler was just rumbling in to the dock. "Do you have a blender, Porter?" she said, when he reached the dock.

Porter took one look at Flipper and raced up to the house with Cathy. It took some doing, but he found the blender in the back of

a cupboard. Cathy produced worms and fish heads and dumped them into it.

"What do you call that?" Porter groaned.

"It's a dolphin shake. Sort of an emergency supply of iron, protein, and other nutrients." She glanced around. "Would you happen to have any gelatin dessert mix?"

Porter found some and dumped it into the blender. When the rich, purple concoction was ready, Cathy slid it into the freezer and slammed the refrigerator door. "We have to give it time to freeze," she explained.

They sat outside and waited. Time seemed to take forever. Finally the dolphin concoction was ready. They took the tray down to Flipper. Cathy pried out a cube and handed it to Sandy.

"It's best from you," she said with an encouraging smile.

Sandy carried the cube into the water. When he reached Flipper, he brought it to Flipper's mouth. But Flipper just lay there. He did not open his mouth. He did not open his eyes. He couldn't move. He was too weak.

"C'mon boy," Sandy coaxed. "You can do it."

Still Flipper did not open his mouth.

"Please, Flipper. Just try. It's so important," Sandy was bent so close to the dolphin that he was practically glued to his skin.

This time Flipper responded. It was a tiny movement at first. Just a shiver. But then his mouth opened. Then it opened a little wider. It wasn't much. But it was enough for Sandy to ease the cube in.

Flipper took the cube. After a few seconds he opened his mouth again. His eyes flickered and tried to focus.

"Keep going," Cathy urged. "Keep feeding him."

Sandy gave Flipper another, and then more and more.

When the cubes were almost gone, everyone laughed in relief. Flipper was already perking up.

Sandy looked up at Cathy. "Is he gonna be OK?"

Cathy nodded. Flipper had returned just in time. The little dolphin was going to be just fine.

Chapter 6

Sandy set up a bed on the dock while Flipper was healing. He needed to be near Flipper while the dolphin was recuperating, still in the hammock sling. Sandy spent nearly every minute of every day at the dock for days on end. He needed to make sure that Flipper was still all right.

One morning a splash woke him. Sandy opened his eyes and glanced into the pen. Flipper's sling was empty. He bolted upright. Then he froze with panic.

Another splash of water caught him and brought him to his feet. Flipper was waiting for him. He wanted to play.

"Flipper!" Sandy cried, jumping gleefully into the water.

"Looks like Flipper's better," Cathy laughed. She was sitting on the porch beside Porter, drinking coffee, and watching Sandy and Flipper frolic in the water.

"How am I going to tell him?" Porter asked. "Flipper is all he cares about."

"You have to. It's the right thing, and you know it," Cathy reminded Porter for the thousandth time. "Even if Flipper needs help, he belongs in the wild."

Before Porter had a chance to answer, a girl on a scooter pulled up in the driveway.

"There's Jan with the test results," Cathy said. "You'd better go talk to Sandy while I see what she found out."

Porter could see that Flipper was feeling much better. The dolphin was out of his sling for good now and had clearly gained weight. When Porter strolled onto the dock, he was tossing a beach ball back to Sandy.

"Talk to you a sec?" Porter asked Sandy.

"Sure. What's up?"

"Do you love Flipper?"

Sandy frowned. What was this all about? "Well, yeah."

"Flipper belongs with the other dolphins, Sandy. You've loved him. You've rescued him. Now it's time to give him back the rest of his life."

"Wait a minute! What's this? He's happy here!" Sandy insisted.

"Of course he is," Porter said gently. "He's very happy. But that doesn't mean it's the best thing for him."

Sandy didn't know what to say. He moved away from Porter to silently watch Flipper.

Cathy joined them. "Looks like Flipper was a lot more than dehydrated," she said. "He was poisoned. The tests showed levels of Dioxin off the chart for these waters. Another meal out there, and he'd be glowing."

"Someone poisoned him?" Sandy couldn't believe what he was hearing. "Why would somebody do that?"

"Or poisoned the water," Cathy explained.

Porter paced the dock and thought about it. "I don't get it. The nearest industry's on the mainland."

"Maybe the mainland's found a cheap place to dump their garbage," Cathy suggested. She studied Porter. She knew her words would disgust him. He loved these waters. And there was nothing he despised more than people who trashed them.

Suddenly Sandy remembered something. "Last night Kim and I went out in the dinghy looking for Flipper. Dirk Moran's boat was out there. We saw some guys tossing barrels or something over the side."

Porter's eyes narrowed. "Did they see you?"

"I don't think so."

"Do you remember where you were?" Cathy asked.

Sandy nodded. How could he forget it? He had searched every inch of that area when he was looking for Flipper.

"OK," Cathy said, as she jumped into the trawler. "Show us."

"Wait," Sandy said. "Let me call Kim. There were two of us then. There should be two of us now."

They didn't have to wait long. When Kim arrived, they sped out into the open sea and slowed down.

It took them a long time to find the exact spot, and Porter was annoyed.

"It was dark," Sandy explained. "It's not like there were street signs or anything."

"Could you see the lighthouse? Any buoys?" Porter probed.

"I'm pretty sure this was the basic spot," Kim said.

Porter slammed his fist on the boat and groaned.

"Come on Porter," Cathy said. "Give them a break, will you? We're all on the same side here."

Porter shook his head and took a deep breath. When he was calm, he apologized. "I'm just a little upset," he admitted. "See, if this is where you were last night, then Dirk Moran's been dumping poison on my fishing grounds."

Sandy nodded and slid down in the back of the boat. Porter took one last look around and turned the boat toward home. Sandy's stomach churned as they moved through the swells. But he managed to keep his dinner down.

Porter was feeling sick, too. But it was a different kind of sickness.

As he looked out at his beloved ocean, a deep sadness gripped his soul.

✦ ✦ ✦

Porter and Cathy found Buck Cowan in The Barnacle.

"We gotta talk, Buck!" Porter said,

"It's my day off," Buck said.

"We think we know why the fishing's been so lousy," Porter said slowly.

"Somebody may be criminally poisoning these waters," Cathy added. "When Flipper came back sick, I did some tests—"

"You mean that dolphin's back?"

Cathy and Porter glanced at each other and frowned. "Hear us out, Buck!" Porter said. "Somebody's dumping Dioxin in these waters. Someone's poisoning these fish!"

Cathy pulled out the lab report and handed it over. "You've got to do something. Look at these results."

But Buck wasn't having it. "Computer printouts don't interest me," he said. "Bring me some hard evidence that somebody's dumping, and I'll bust 'em. Until then, we've got a dolphin situation on our hands. Do you have any idea how many marine parks I've turned away since that dolphin's shown up? An animal smart as that makes a fine attraction. If Flipper's still here on Monday, I'll personally see to it he's jumping through flaming hoops at Sea World on Tuesday."

Cathy and Porter walked out of The Barnacle. Their minds raced as they tried to figure out what to do. Sandy and Kim were waiting for them in the trawler. Cathy explained the situation.

"Look," she said. "We still have until Monday. That gives us three days to deploy our secret weapon." She pointed toward Flipper and grinned.

"Him?" Porter said. "How?"

"Project Quick Find. The Navy started playing with it after the Korean War. They trained dolphins to find things on the ocean

floor. Spy satellites, enemy subs, junk like that. It was top secret till a few years ago," Cathy explained, the plan forming in her mind as the words came out of her mouth. "So let's go. We've got work to do."

Porter glanced over at Sandy. He wondered if his nephew was thinking about the concert on Saturday night. There was no way they were going to make it. He tried to think of a kind way to tell him. But there was no nice way to say it. He'd just have to give it to him straight.

"Guess we're gonna miss that concert," Porter said gently.

Sandy shrugged. "What concert?" Then he untied the trawler rope and tossed it into the boat.

☼ ☼ ☼

At six the following morning, they were back in the trawler. They weren't going anywhere. They were just getting Flipper ready for his tour of duty.

"Flipper's secret can be summed up in one word," Cathy explained. "Echolocation."

"Echo what?" Kim asked.

Cathy grinned. "Dolphin sonar. Flipper sends a beam of sound towards an object and receives an echo back. He can see in total darkness."

"He's great at finding loose change," Sandy laughed.

"Like a dog," Kim added. "But instead of his nose, he looks with his echo thing."

Cathy leaned over the dock and placed some rubber suction eye-cups over Flipper's eyes. Then she skipped a quarter into the water.

"Go get it, Flipper!" she called.

Flipper dove. In seconds, he was back with the quarter.

"But there's more," Cathy said. "He may find something too big to bring up. So he'll need to tell us about it. I'm going to rig up a tennis ball over the water. Sandy, it's your job to teach him to tap the ball every time he finds something. And don't forget his stamina.

Run him ragged until he's able to keep up with us. He's got a big job ahead of him."

Chapter 6

Sandy and Flipper spent the next day in training. As Sandy jogged along the coast road, Flipper swam nearby. They moved slowly at first. Then Sandy sped up, and Flipper stayed right with him. Sandy tried to go faster, pump harder, pushing frantically. But the little dolphin outdid him. It was Sandy who needed work on his stamina, not Flipper. No matter how hard Sandy pumped, Flipper stayed ahead.

Sandy switched from foot to bike. But that was no good either. Flipper was just too fast for him. Even a moped couldn't beat him. The dolphin was a winner. And it was time to take him out to sea. He was ready.

"I think we've got everything," Cathy said the next morning as they were loading the trawler. "Hydrophone, decompression chamber."

"Zinc oxide, Blistex, and . . ." Porter reached over and tried to stick a seasickness prevention patch on Sandy's temple.

But Sandy wouldn't have it. He swatted him away. "What are you doing?"

"It's a nausea prevention patch," Porter told him in a whisper. "Do you want to lose your lunch in front of her?" He nodded in Kim's direction.

Sandy glanced over at Kim huddled with Cathy over the supply box. He thought about it for a moment. Then he took the patch and slapped it on.

He settled in beside Marvin and grinned. "Like your shorts," he said. Marvin's shorts were getting brighter and busier by the day.

"Wait a minute," Cathy said. "One more thing." She jumped out of the boat and grabbed the inflatable dinghy and tied it to the stern. "Just in case," she laughed. "You never know in situations like these."

When she was back on board, Porter gunned the engine and they were on their way.

Flipper was ready. He stayed with the boat the whole way, even when Porter sped it up. When they reached their destination, he swam closer and waited.

"OK!" Cathy called. "First things first. Porter, you can keep track of Flipper's progress so we don't cover the same ground. You can handle it. It's just a computer."

Porter groaned and went below. When he was gone Cathy turned to Kim. "Why don't you spot, Kim? And Marvin, this is for you." She handed him a box marked FRAGILE and waited as he took it down to the cabin. "You can help Porter get that computer going."

"Now," she said when Marvin was gone. "Let's see what this dolphin can do. This one's up to you, Sandy."

Sandy spread out on his belly and flicked some water at Flipper. "Go on, Flipper!" he said.

Flipper turned and dove deep into the water. When he emerged, he ignored the tennis ball that Cathy had rigged up over the water. He dove again, then again and again, but each time he came up he ignored the ball.

The trawler moved through the water slowly as the humans waited for the dolphin to find what they were looking for. Hours passed. Still Flipper found nothing. They were about to give up when Flipper rocketed out of the water and tapped the tennis ball.

Sandy jumped to his feet. "I think he found something!"

They came together and watched the spot where they had last seen Flipper. Suddenly he splashed to the surface and jumped. Again and again, he jumped over the same spot.

"He's definitely found something!" Sandy called, as the trawler moved closer to Flipper.

Sandy tossed him some reward fish and waited as Cathy called down to Marvin. In a minute, Marvin came up with a very strange contraption that looked like a video camera.

"He worked so hard," Cathy said, patting Marvin on the shoulders as she explained to everyone else what he had made. "The Navy spent millions, and Marv did it with fifty bucks. It's got everything: camera, underwater housing, and a bite plate for Flipper to carry it."

"That's great, Marv!" Sandy said. Flipper took the bite plate into his mouth. Then they watched together as the little dolphin flipped his tail and disappeared. When he was gone, they went below and followed his progress on the video monitor.

"Where's he going?" Sandy asked.

"I don't see anything," Kim told him.

Sandy was the first to see the dolphins. There was a whole pod of them. They were gathered around the camera.

"Maybe that's Flipper's family," Sandy said. "I hope he doesn't stop."

Flipper didn't stop. He kept right on going, until he was almost to the bottom.

"What's that stuff?" Kim asked.

She moved closer to the monitor. "It looks like dead fish. Lots and lots of dead fish. And . . . wait a minute! What's that?"

"Fifty-five gallon drums," Cathy said. "There must be hundreds of them."

As Flipper swam closer, the group began to make out the words on the drums: DANGER: TOXIC WASTE.

"Gross!" Kim cried.

"We'd better get ahold of Buck," Cathy suggested.

But Porter had a better idea. "This is truly horrible! How about the Environmental Protection Agency? Or the FBI. Or the Coast Guard!"

Cathy grabbed the radio. "Ship to shore," she announced. "This is Cathy Simms for Coast Guard. Come in!" But there was no answer. And when she tried again, there was still no answer.

Dirk Moran had intercepted the call and he wasn't wasting time. The words were hardly out of Cathy's mouth when he turned a knob in the cabin of the *Bounty Hunter*. Her voice faded under a blanket of static. And then it disappeared altogether.

Moran had locked the frequency.

"What the—?" Porter said. "The radio was working yesterday."

"How come the picture stopped moving?" Sandy asked.

But no one was listening to him. They were too busy setting a flashing-red radio beacon over the site.

"This'll send out a radio signal so we can find the spot again," Cathy explained. "Now we'd better go in."

"I'm not going!" Sandy announced. "I'm not leaving without Flipper. Something's wrong. I'll stay with the dinghy, and when I find him, I'll come in."

"No!" Porter said, glaring. He was not about to leave Sandy behind. They spent a few minutes cleaning up and preparing the equipment for their departure.

But when the trawler moved away, Sandy was in the dinghy, hiding. And no one was aware that he was gone.

When the boat was out of sight, Sandy yelled, "Flipper! Flipper!" He rowed over to the beacon and gazed into the water. There was no sign of Flipper anywhere. And just what was that loud, rumbling . . .

He looked around just in time to see the huge hull of the *Bounty Hunter* coming straight toward him. There was no time to think. In seconds he would be dead if he didn't do something fast!

Sandy leapt into the water and swam away, as the *Bounty Hunter* bore down on the tiny dinghy and destroyed it in a crash of splintering material.

The huge boat sped up and moved on, leaving Sandy with one small part of the dinghy to hold onto. One of the oars was still attached.

He closed his eyes and took a deep breath. After a moment, he opened them again. A dorsal fin was circling nearby. Sandy grinned. Everything was going to be all right.

"Flipper!" Sandy called. "I'm over here Flipper!"

But the fin was too big. This couldn't be Flipper. It had to be something bigger. Sandy shivered, and then he remembered what Kim had told him about the hammerhead ages ago when they had first met by the dock. The fin belonged to Scar, the most dreaded shark in that part of the sea.

Sandy kicked his feet, moving backward. Then he grabbed for the oar that was still attached to the crushed dinghy.

"Flipper?" he called hoarsely. "Flipper?"

Flipper saw the shark before he heard Sandy's voice. The dolphin was backtracking away through the water when Sandy called again.

It was a terrible scream. A scream of complete terror. The shark had broken water and was heading straight toward the boy. The shark's huge jaws were opening wide. He was circling closer. In a moment he would be on him.

Sandy raised the oar.

Scar chomped on the oar instead of Sandy. Then he disappeared into the depths again. But the hammerhead was not about to give up so easily. He emerged again quickly, jaws agape, ready to attack. But this time Flipper was there. The little dolphin came in from the side, and rammed the hammerhead hard. Over and over, as Scar circled back toward Sandy, the little dolphin rammed him.

Sandy glanced away just for a second to see the returning boat.

The *Bounty Hunter* was moving toward the beacon. Someone was leaning over the side and plucking it from the water. It was Dirk Moran, and he had spotted him.

Moran waved him toward the boat. Sandy raced toward it, kicking his feet frantically, and he did not look back. Not once. Not until he was on the ladder. And then, only then, did he turn and to look over his shoulder. He couldn't believe what he was seeing.

Flipper's family had come to his rescue. They circled the mammoth shark and rammed him until they had won the mighty battle. Then they chased him away.

"That is one courageous little dolphin," Dirk said menacingly as Sandy started to climb up the ladder.

Sandy reached the top and glanced up. Dirk's eyes were dark and narrow. In his hand was the long iron pole that he had used to retrieve the beacon.

"I'm sorry you had to see us that night," Dirk growled.

Sandy took another step up and hesitated. Moran was raising the pole. He was glowering down at him. He raised the pole higher, then higher still.

Sandy saw it coming. He knew that Moran was aiming for his head. He closed his eyes.

When nothing happened, he opened them again and glanced over his shoulder. Flipper was behind him, exploding out of the water. With one blow, he slapped Moran with his tail and sent him sprawling into the water.

Chapter 10

P orter saw it happen. It hadn't taken long to discover that Sandy was no longer with them. They had immediately turned back. They had made good time, but they weren't fast enough to save him from the water shark—or the human shark. Flipper had done that for them.

"You all right?" Porter asked as he scooped Sandy out of the water. When his nephew was on board, he gave him a concerned once-over. Then he hugged him. It was just a quick little hug. But it was enough to make Sandy uncomfortable. He wiggled away and slid down in the boat.

"I'm fine," he muttered. Then he glanced over at Kim. "Remember that story about Scar? Well, it's true."

Behind them, Dirk was bobbing in the water. Porter grinned. This was going to be fun. He leaned over and pulled him out. Then he shoved him right back in and tossed him a life preserver.

"What if the hammerhead comes back?" Moran pleaded. "I'm a sitting duck! You can't leave me here."

"Don't worry," Porter laughed. "If he takes a bite out of you, I'm sure he'll spit it out."

But Dirk wasn't listening. He was too busy screaming. Because a dorsal fin was moving straight toward him.

"Help!" Dirk shouted. "Get me out of here! Help!"

The little group on the trawler laughed. They knew who it was. The fin was too small to belong to a shark. This fish wasn't the hammerhead. It was Flipper. And he was hosing Dirk right between the eyes!

⚙ ⚙ ⚙

Sandy was surprised to see that Buck was waiting for them when they got to the dock. Porter handed Dirk over to the Coast Guard, and Buck shook Porter's hand.

"Wait a minute," Sandy said. "I thought you couldn't get through. I thought the radio was busted."

"We finally got through to Buck here," Porter began.

"I got in touch with the Coast Guard," Buck added. "And they've been out there. It's a mess. But it looks like we caught it before too much toxic waste leaked out."

"Thanks for that," Porter said and sighed. Sandy knew he was relieved. "Who knows what would have happened to the fish and plants around there? Just a little bit of that waste killed an awful lot of fish. I just wonder who Moran was working for."

"Probably a factory on the mainland that makes weed killers. They had to get rid of their garbage somehow. So why not use Moran? The Environmental Protection Agency's on their way," Buck said. "We'll get it cleaned up. Thanks to Flipper."

"What about Flipper?" Sandy asked. "Can I keep him? He saved my life out there."

Buck rubbed his chin pensively. After a while he said the words that Sandy had been waiting so long to hear. "Well," he said. "As long as he's free, then I guess he's free to make this his home. And we'll have a pretty nifty dolphin looking out for us."

But for some reason, Sandy didn't seem happy about that. He walked away and stood alone, gazing out at the sea. After a moment he returned. "He should go," he said.

Everyone turned and stared at Sandy.

"He belongs with his family," Sandy muttered.

Near the dock, Flipper was chattering. It was as if he wanted to be part of the conversation. Sandy knelt down, and Flipper moved closer. Sandy reached out his hand, and Flipper rose up to meet him. At that moment, Sandy and Flipper touched for the very last time. Then Sandy said the words that he thought he would never say. "Go on, boy."

But the dolphin didn't go. He yipped and nodded and rose up into the air. Then he looked up and waited.

Sandy understood. "No," he said. "I can't come. Now go on. It's OK. I'll be all right. And so will you. GO!"

Flipper moved slowly away. When he had gone a few yards, he circled back and stared up at Sandy one last time. Then he turned and sailed through the water. As the tiny fin moved out to sea, a pod of dolphins rose up in the distance. They soared into the air. Then they moved in and waited while Flipper came to them.

Flipper and his family dove and played together for a long time. Then they swam away and disappeared.

✹ ✹ ✹

The next day, Sandy, too, joined his family. They arrived at Porter's in a rental car, and for some reason his mom seemed shy.

"Hello, Sandy," his mom said.

"Hi, Mom." Sandy said. He moved toward his mom and put his arms around her. He hugged her tightly. When he let her go, she stood very still. She was stunned. That hug was the one thing she hadn't expected—and it was a wonderful surprise.

"So how was your summer?" his sister asked.

"It was a total blast. It was the best ever."

His mom smiled and glanced over at Porter. "Well, I can hardly wait to hear about it," she said. And we'll have plenty of time, too. I thought you and Hannah and I could drive up north together. Sort of make a trip of it. It'll be nice to spend some time together."

"Sounds great," Sandy said. And everyone could tell that he meant it.

Porter, Kim, Marvin, and Cathy went down to the ferry with Sandy, his mom, and his sister to say a proper goodbye. Marvin was wearing an even wilder pair of boxers, and he seemed especially proud of them. Sandy went over to him and smiled.

"See you around, Marv," he said.

But Marvin didn't smile back. At first Sandy thought Marvin was sad because he was leaving.

"What's the matter?" Sandy asked.

"Flipper."

"He'll be back. You just wait and see."

It was hard for Sandy to leave them all. He felt all choked up when both Cathy and Kim gave him a hug goodbye. But it was especially hard to say goodbye to Porter. He couldn't think of the right thing to say, so he didn't say anything. He just hugged his uncle, and then he turned and walked onto the ferry.

When he was settled in his seat, he leaned back and thought about his summer. It had been a good one. The best summer so far. He would come back to this island. He was sure about that.

Someone was laughing on the other side of the ferry. The laughter was coming from the railing. There were lots of people gathered there. They were pointing at something in the water. Sandy stood and walked over. He looked down. And then he smiled.

It was Flipper. Far below, in the dark sea, the little dolphin was dancing. When he saw Sandy, he rose up and yipped. Sandy waved, and Flipped yipped again.

On the dock, Marvin saw Flipper, too. His voice rose above the sound of the ferry's engines. "Flipper!" Marvin called. "Flipper!"

Sandy turned and waved to Marvin. Then he leaned against the rail and watched as his friend Flipper escorted the ferry out to sea.